P9-CFF-685

For my horsey friend Evie —A. L.
For Annabel, for the horse poses —R. H.

First published in the United States in 2009 by Chronicle Books LLC.

Text © 2007 by Alison Lester.
Illustrations © 2007 by Roland Harvey.
Originally published in Australia in 2007 by Allen & Unwin under the
title *The Shadow Brumby*.

North American type design by David Habben.
Typeset in Berkeley.
Manufactured in China.

Library of Congress Cataloging-in-Publication Data
Lester, Alison.
[Shadow brumby]
The silver horse switch / by Alison Lester ; illustrated by Roland Harvey.
p. cm. — (Horse crazy ; bk. 1)
Summary: In a rural Australian town, best friends Bonnie and Sam, who
share a mutual love of horses, watch in amazement as a farm horse and a
wild horse, identical in appearance, trade places.
ISBN 978-0-8118-6554-8
[1. Horses—Fiction. 2. Friendship—Fiction. 3. Australia—Fiction.]
I. Harvey, Roland, ill. II. Title. III. Series.
PZ7.L56284Si 2009
[Fic]—dc22
2008021973

10 9 8 7 6 5 4 3 2 1

Chronicle Books LLC
680 Second Street, San Francisco, California 94107

www.chroniclekids.com

HORSE crazy

THE SILVER HORSE SWITCH 1

by Alison Lester

illustrated by Roland Harvey

chronicle books · san francisco

Bonnie and Sam

Bonnie and Sam knew all the horses and ponies in Currawong Creek. They were horse crazy!

Sam's real name was Samantha. She lived with her dad, Bill, in an old house that overlooked the creek. Bill Cooper was the local policeman.

Sam

Bonnie

Pants

Bonnie—Bon for short—lived just outside town on a huge farm called Peppermint Plain. Bon's parents weren't interested in horses, even though Peppermint Plain was the perfect place for riding. Her mom, Woo, was a painter, always busy in her studio. Her dad, Chester, loved riding around the farm on his motorbike.

But Bonnie and Sam lived for horses.

Bonnie could talk a special horse language that she was sure they understood.

Sam was strong and horsey. She could tell, just by looking at a horse, if it had a stone in its hoof or needed a drink.

Sam's dog, Pants, followed her everywhere. Pants was short for Smartie Pants, because she thought she knew everything.

The Horses and Ponies of Currawong Creek

Bonnie and Sam didn't have a horse of their own, but they managed to ride nearly every day.

Their favorite horse was Whale, who belonged to Bon's Aunty Birdy. Whale was huge. He was long and wide and tall. He was so broad that Bonnie and Sam could sit face-to-face and play poker on his back.

Whale shared his paddock with Bella, a tiny skewbald pony whose mane came down to her knees. When Sam sat on Bella, she could reach the ground with both big toes. Bella had been Bonnie's first pony, but the girls were far too big to ride her now. Instead, they spent hours grooming her and braiding her mane.

Then there was Biscuit, the most neglected horse in Currawong Creek. Wally Webster, the stock agent, hated horses but he needed poor

Whale

Bella

Biscuit for his stock work. If Bonnie and Sam
hadn't checked her feed and water every day, she
would have died long ago. Biscuit was frightened
of Wally's rough ways and bellowing voice, so
Wally depended on the girls to catch her for him.
In return, they could ride her whenever they
wanted.

Biscuit

Chocolate Charm was another favorite. Her owner, Cheryl Smythe-Tyght, lived near the stock-yards on a property that looked like a toy farm. It had perfect white fences, red sheds, and neat rows of trees with every leaf in place. Choco was a dressage horse: beautiful, well-educated, and obedient. Sometimes Sam and Bonnie picked up horse poo in Cheryl's paddocks in exchange for riding lessons. Trotting around Cheryl's property on the fabulous Choco was the closest thing to heaven the girls had ever known.

Then there were Blondie and Tex, who came to Currawong Creek when their owners, Janice and Bob, took over the newsstand.

Blondie was an elderly quarter horse with a butterscotch coat and a sparkling white mane and tail. Every now and then something would remind her of her sad past, and she'd go all nervous and spooky. Bon could whisper to Blondie in secret horse language and calm her down.

Tex was an ugly Appaloosa with a very sweet nature. He adored Blondie. Nothing bothered Tex, not even when Bob dressed him up as a reindeer last Christmas and threw presents to the little kids waiting outside the newsstand.

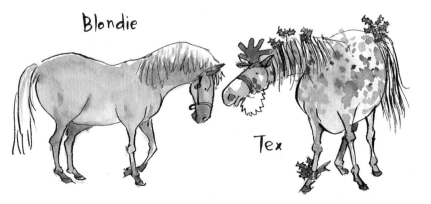

Blondie

Tex

Horrie

Prince Regent, known as Horrie, was Currawong Creek's one and only racehorse. He hadn't won a race for years, but his owner, Bugsy Brady, believed he still had it in him. Horrie was as skittish as a cat and saw spooks in every shadow. Sometimes, Bon and Sam gave him a neck massage on their way home from school. It always put him to sleep.

Tricky was a piebald pony, with a black-and-white personality to match his coloring. He was either very, very good or very, very bad. At pony club, he often played tricks on Michael, his owner. Tricky was the best games pony around, as nimble as a monkey, but if he felt like playing, he was a disaster.

Tricky was devoted to Sam, who never walked past his paddock without stopping to adjust his fly veil or share her apple.

Tricky

The grumpiest pony in Currawong Creek was Tarzan. He was a shaggy buckskin who lived in the paddock next to the primary school. Children had teased him for so long that he chased anyone who came near. Only Sam was brave enough to stand her ground, with Bonnie hiding behind her. Tarzan knew that the girls always brought a treat to make him happy.

Bonnie and Sam could ride all the horses, often bareback and double-dinking. Whenever there was time, the girls borrowed a horse and went riding.

Sometimes in the mountains they caught a glimpse of the wild bush horses—the brumbies. They looked so wild and free, yet Sam and Bonnie couldn't help dreaming about catching a yearling and taming it.

What they didn't know was that one night, while they were still dreaming, a brumby would come to them . . .

Tarzan

13

DROVER

Sam sat on the back porch and watched her
dad's new horse, Drover, pacing up and down
the fence.

"Why's she so unhappy, Pants?"

The little dog whined softly, as if to say,
She's unhappy because she hates being locked up.

Drover's head was turned toward the hills. You could tell she wanted to be there.

Sam called out, "Drover! Dro-ver!" but the silver gray mare didn't even look her way.

Pants rubbed against Sam's leg and made her special snuffly noises that meant, *Look at me! I want to be here.*

Sam scratched her wiry coat. "I know you're happy. But Drover just wants to run away."

The reason Drover hated being locked in a small paddock was that she had spent all her life on the open road. She was a drover's horse. Sam's dad had a mate called Smithy who caught Drover as a two-year-old brumby and broke her in. She grew up to be quick, clever, and calm. Smithy loved her. But one night he camped near railroad tracks and Drover was nearly hit by a train. She wasn't hurt, but, after that night, every time she heard or saw a train, she bolted.

"She runs like the devil's after her," Smithy explained when he brought Drover to Currawong Creek. "I can't use her any more because I often work near a train line."

Sam's heart did a little somersault. Maybe he was going to give the horse to her!

"But you could use her, Bill. There's no train line here. She'd be perfect for your police work. And her hard little hooves never need shoes."

Sam's face dropped and Smithy guessed what she had been hoping.

"I'm sorry, Sam. I know you'd love your own horse, but this one's not for you. She's definitely not a kid's horse."

Drover turned out to be an excellent police horse. Bill could catch her any time, day or night, and she'd do whatever he asked.

It didn't bother Bill that she was unfriendly and restless in her paddock. He just wanted a horse that did the job, and Drover did.

Together, Bill and Drover herded Wally Webster's sheep back into their paddock when they wandered through the town in the middle of the night. They did it so quietly that Mrs. Green never knew what had eaten her roses and gladioli.

When Tom Morgan's bad-tempered bull went rampaging through town, Bill and Drover stopped him. Bill cracked his whip and Drover ducked away from the bull's fearsome horns. Together they forced the brute back to his yard.

And when Mrs. Kowalski's kitten got stuck up a tree, Drover stood steady while Bill fetched her down.

"She's the best horse I've ever owned," Bill said to Sam. "I've had her for three weeks now and she hasn't put a foot wrong."

But Drover wasn't a great horse for Bonnie and Sam.

One Saturday afternoon when Bill was away, they decided to ride her. The girls were used to all the Currawong Creek horses liking them. Not Drover. When she bucked Sam off, they thought Sam's jump-up had frightened her. But when Bonnie slid gently on from a stump, the same thing happened. A swish of mane, a stamp of hooves, and Bonnie was on the ground. The girls both tried until they were sore and sick of it.

"And look." Bonnie went to hug Drover, but the mare pulled away. "She doesn't even like us touching her."

Sam pulled off her helmet and rubbed at a grass stain on it. "Smithy said she wasn't a kid's horse. Maybe she's only been ridden by grown-ups, and we seem a bit weird."

"Maybe a kid did something mean and gave her that moon-shaped scar under her mane."

Bonnie rolled up the leg of her jeans to inspect her own scar. "Oh well, I guess it's like people. Not everyone wants to be your friend."

SHADOW

Late one night, Shadow the silver brumby
slipped through the eucalyptus trees, racing to
catch up with the mob.

She hated being last. Everywhere Shadow
looked, she saw danger. The other wild horses
trotted happily through the moonlit bush, but
Shadow was afraid.

Shadow had been born on a farm where she
felt safe and secure. Then one day her mother

pushed open a broken gate and took Shadow into the mountains, following the call of the brumbies. From then on, Shadow was always tense and worried.

Storms were Shadow's greatest fear. She hated the terrifying crash of thunder, and the lightning that tore through Wild Dog Range. Most of all, she hated being afraid.

Now the stallion who led the brumbies plunged down the mountain, scattering rocks, with the mob close behind. The smell of smoke and humans drifted through the trees. He was leading them to the town!

The brumbies trotted silently across the river flats. Lights glowed yellow through the mist, and a dog barked, *Arf, arf, arf.* They slowed to a walk, reaching down to snatch bites of sweet green grass.

The stallion stopped still, quivering, ears forward. Then he pranced up to a fence and Shadow saw what had lured him from the mountains. A beautiful silver gray mare stood neck-to-neck with the brumby stallion, breathing his scent.

That mare was Drover.

Suddenly the mare squealed and spun around, kicking. The stallion backed away and led his mob further along the creek. But Shadow stopped to stare at Drover. It was as though she were seeing her own reflection. They were identical.

The two silver gray
mares moved to the fence,
like dancers coming together.
Shadow gazed into the paddock with
its shade trees, water trough, and stable,
so comfortable and safe. Drover looked past
Shadow at the brumbies grazing by the river,
free to race back to their wild mountain home.
Both horses saw the life they wanted, with
only the fence in their way.

25

The stallion trotted back from the creek, snorting and driving Shadow away. With a fierce cry he led the mob back into the hills, leaving Drover alone in her paddock.

The sound of the wild horses disappearing into the bush made Drover feel as if she were in jail. Her hooves kicked up tiny puffs of dust as she paced along the fence. Her ears strained to hear the brumbies. One set of hoof beats sounded strangely close . . . closer . . . Then, like a ghost appearing from darkness, Shadow burst out of the night and trotted up to Drover.

Neck-to-neck they stood, nuzzling each other's withers. Then Shadow wheeled away, cantered back, and flew over the fence like a bird.

Drover's heart lifted as the brumby jumped into her paddock. It looked so easy, so effortless. She knew she could do it too.

Shadow and Drover danced together, twisting and spinning in the moonlight. If Sam had looked out of her bedroom window just then, she would have thought she was dreaming.

The horses cantered in a circle, side-by-side. Then Shadow peeled away while Drover raced straight for the fence, soared over with room to spare, whinnied, and galloped away into the night.

Shadow turned and looked around her new paddock. She gave a sigh and felt a delicious peace come over her. She was home.

New Drover

Bill Cooper finished his cup of tea and glanced out at the paddock. "Look, Drover's finally stopped pacing up and down! I don't believe it. She's snoozing by the shed."

Sam and Bonnie went to see if Drover really had calmed down. They walked slowly, calling her name and softly holding out an apple as a peace offering. The horse stared at them, head up, snorting, eyes nearly popping out of her head.

"What's happened to her?" Bon was puzzled. "She normally just ignores us, but she's acting as if we're Martians. Look, she's trembling like a leaf."

The mare didn't turn her rump to them in her usual unfriendly way. Instead, she moved forward slowly. Then, very cautiously, she nuzzled Bon's neck.

Bon giggled and put her arms around the mare's neck. Drover leaned into her as though she loved it.

"This is very weird," said Sam, rubbing the horse's ears. "She looks the same, but she's behaving so different."

Bon put her nose right on Drover's gray coat and sniffed. "She even smells different. She smells of the bush."

The two girls went over the horse like detectives, looking for clues. They found that, overnight, Bill's horse had developed a matted mane and tail, cracked hooves, and a couple of new scars on her legs. The crescent-shaped scar under her mane had disappeared.

"You're not Drover," said Bon, shaking her head. "You're somebody else!"

"I'd better tell Dad."

"Hang on, Sammy." Bon was untangling the mare's mane. "She loves us. Maybe we shouldn't tell him. Drover was never this friendly."

"She is nice," Sam agreed, "but Dad's bound to find out anyway. Look at her hooves."

"We could trim them, and comb the knots out of her mane. He'll never notice."

"But who swapped her? It's not fair to Dad. They must think he's too stupid to know his own horse."

"Mmmnn, that's something to think about."
Bon crinkled up her eyes the way she always
did when she had a problem. "Let's check the
bottom fence."

The mare followed, nudging them gently with
her nose. They expected to find the fence cut,
but it looked the same as ever.

Sam wriggled carefully through the barbed
wire and bent down, studying the ground. "A
lot of horses have been here, and none of them
were wearing shoes." She looked at Bon proudly.
"You know what that means?"

"Brumbies! Maybe Drover has gone off with
the brumbies. And maybe this horse is a
brumby who decided to stay. Oh, please don't
tell your dad, Sam, not right away anyhow.
Let's just see how she turns out."

THE MAKEOVER

The new Drover was a quick learner. She stood
as still as stone while Bonnie and Sam took
turns with the big hoof rasp. They filed off the
broken bits until the new mare's hooves were as
smooth and round as the old Drover's.

Everything was new to her. As the day went
by, the girls became more and more convinced
that their "brumby swap" theory was right.

When they put a headstall on her, she snorted
and looked surprised, but didn't back away.
Whenever she seemed afraid, Bonnie soothed her
with secret horse talk and massaged the tension
out of her neck. They combed all the knots out
of her mane and tail, then trimmed the bottom
of her tail square, like they'd done with old
Drover. Then they washed her and brushed her
as she dried in the sunshine.

"I don't think your dad will be able to tell the difference." Bon stared at their handiwork from the shade of the old eucalyptus tree. "She looks just the same."

"Yep." Sam fondled Pants's ears. "She looks the same. But when he rides her, he'll notice."

Bonnie and Sam decided they needed help. An unbroken brumby would be hard to train, no matter how friendly she was. They called on someone they could trust—Birdy Davidson. Aunty Birdy never treated them like little kids, and she knew everything there was to know about horses.

When the girls told her about Drover and the brumby, she nodded. "It sounds as though you're right about the swap. Horses have a mind of their own, you know."

The three of them sat on the bench on the veranda and watched Birdy's horse Whale grazing in the paddock behind the house.

"Can you tell us how to train her?" Bon asked. "She won't know anything about being ridden."

Sam squirmed in her chair. She still didn't feel good about tricking her father.

"We've only got five days. Dad always rides through the town on Thursdays. And it takes ages to break in a horse, doesn't it?"

"Well, it depends on the horse," answered
Birdy. "Look at Whale. He's such a sweet-
natured horse that he almost trained himself.
Your brumby sounds the same. Let's go and have
a look at her."

Over the next five days, whenever Bill Cooper
was away from home, Birdy and the girls worked
on the new Drover.

On the first day they taught her to lead. Sam walked beside the mare, gently encouraging her forward. When Sam stopped, Drover stopped. When Sam walked, Drover walked, too. Then Sam ran slowly and the brumby trotted beside her.

Birdy smiled. She liked the look of this horse and her gentle eye. "Now make her go backward," she said to Sam. "It's important she knows to yield to you."

Sam held the rope close to the headstall and pushed steadily away. Drover stepped carefully back. "Good girl," soothed Sam. "Good horse."

On the second day they taught her to tie up and accept the saddle. Sam put the saddle blanket on Drover's back, then carefully placed Bill's heavy stock saddle on top. Drover jumped slightly and then looked embarrassed. Her reactions were the same with every step: at first she was frightened, but she quickly took to things.

On the third day they put her bridle on. She mouthed the bit at first as though she'd tasted something really bad, but soon started chewing on it. "That's good," said Birdy. "That means she's accepted it."

On the fourth day they drove her in long reins, making sure she knew which way to go and when to stop.

On the fifth day it was time to get on. When Sam swung up into the saddle, new Drover turned her head and stared in amazement. Bon patted her neck and soothed her, then Sam squeezed her legs and the horse stepped forward. Birdy and Bon watched them go around the paddock, walking, circling left, circling right, sideways, backward.

Finally Sam pushed Drover into a canter. They turned and trotted back up to where Birdy and Bon were sitting. Sam swung out of the saddle. She was beaming.

"She's beautiful, isn't she? Have a ride, Bon, you'll love her. I think she's going to be okay."

THE TEST DRIVE

The next day, Sam's dad got ready for his weekly tour of the town.

"Please don't do anything stupid," Sam whispered into new Drover's ear.

Drover gave a little snort of surprise as Bill swung into the saddle and his full weight settled on her back.

Bill turned to ride out the gate and Drover didn't respond. Old Drover would have felt the shift of his body and moved off, but new Drover just stood still. Bill had to squeeze with his legs to make her go. Sam quickly went to her head and led her through the gate.

"What's gotten into her?" said Bill. "She's acting like a drongo." He turned the mare towards the town and kicked her forward. Sam crossed her fingers.

"Have a lovely ride, Dad. Don't fall off." Sam bit her lip. "He thinks I'm joking," she said to Pants.

Sergeant Bill Cooper loved riding through town. It was a good way to keep in touch with people. He saw all sorts of things from the back of his horse that he'd never see from his car. He always took the same route, so nobody thought he was sneaking around. But today, his horse's mind was not on the job. She wobbled and weaved as though she had no idea where she was going, and stared at everything. Bill had to ride her like a green horse that knew nothing.

39

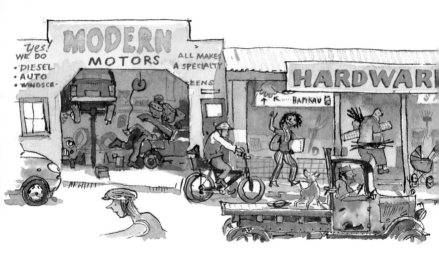

"Hey, Bill!" Mick Daly, the baker, called from over the street. "I want to ask you something."

Bill steered Drover across, expecting her to stop just in front of Mick. But Drover walked right up close until Mick's face was pressed against her mane.

"Whoa there, horse," said Mick, stepping back. "Hasn't she heard about personal space?"

"I don't know what the story is, mate. She's acting very strangely."

The two men chatted for a while, but when Mick walked back inside his bakery, Drover followed him right into the shop. Bill had to duck quickly to fit under the doorway. Drover stopped at the counter and Bill looked down at Mrs. Bowman, who was putting a poppy-seed loaf into her basket.

"I don't think the health inspector would approve of a horse in a food store," Mrs. Bowman sniffed. "Even a police horse." She minced out of the shop with her basket, and Mick burst out laughing.

"It's pretty funny, Bill, but you'd better get her out of here. I could be fined."

41

"I might not be able to keep her after all, Sam," said Bill, watching the mare roll in the paddock after the ride. "She's been such a good horse until now, but today she was a real dodo."

Sam wanted to tell her dad the truth right then, but it was such a big thing to confess. When he told her all the odd things Drover had done, her heart sank.

"Did you laugh when she ate the flowers on Mrs. Milson's hat?" she asked, hanging up the bridle.

"I wanted to. But I had to be serious. I'm the policeman. And I've got a horse that's breaking the law." He picked up Pants and scratched her back. "The trouble is, I don't know if I can trust her. Next weekend I have to take her to the Baxter Show. They want a mounted officer there, and Charlie Craig's horse is lame."

He put Pants down, stretched, and yawned.

"I wish she hadn't started acting so strangely, just when I have to put her to the test. The train line goes through Baxter, right near the showgrounds. What if she freaks out at the two-thirty train?"

Sam patted her dad on the back. "She'll be fine, Dad. I bet you anything she won't worry about the train."

She hurried inside to call Bonnie. This new Drover might do some weird things, but she had no reason to be scared of trains.

THE BAXTER SHOW

Bonnie and Sam led Drover past the Ferris wheel and the bumper cars. Bonnie talked to Drover all the time in her secret horse language. The mare was calm, although she looked wide-eyed at all the action going on around her. People kept stopping to admire her beautiful silver gray coat.

"We're taking her to meet my dad at the cattle sheds," Sam explained for the eighth time.

Drover took a bite from a little boy's cotton candy and Sam and Bonnie quickly led her on.

"I hope she'll be okay, Bon," said Sam. "It would be terrible if something went wrong because of what we've done."

"She'll be fine. Now that she knows your dad, she'll be much better. Look! There he is!"

Bonnie and Sam sat on the arena fence, watching the dressage horses go around and around. Chocolate Charm was in the final for Champion Hack of the Show. She moved through her workout like a well-oiled Rolls Royce, her brown coat shining in the sun, saddlery gleaming. The girls clapped and cheered when the red, white, and blue champion sash was put around Choco's neck.

They were heading for the arena exit when a siren suddenly howled over the loudspeaker.

"Sergeant Bill Cooper! Calling Sergeant Bill Cooper! We have an emergency! Come straight to the tent in the main arena."

Sam watched her father gallop across the ground. "She's going good for him, Bonnie."

It was true, the mare did seem calm and confident.

"You have to help us!" A desperate woman rushed toward Bill. Her eyes were red from crying. "Our little girl has disappeared. She was right beside me, on her trike, and then all of a sudden she was gone!"

Bill quickly took down the details and organized a message over the loudspeaker.

"We have a missing child at the Baxter Show-grounds. Kimberley Mills is two years old and was riding her red plastic tricycle near the Ferris wheel when she disappeared. She has blonde curly hair and is wearing purple overalls and

a white T-shirt. I repeat, we have a missing child . . ."

Bill raced away to search for the little girl. Suddenly there was a scream from behind the showground bathrooms.

Bill galloped Drover around the tumbledown building and there was Kimberley's mother, pointing into the distance. "There she is!"

Behind a hedge of blackberries was a lane, and right at the end of it was a small purple figure.

"Can you see? That's her! I know it's her!"

"You'd better be quick," said an elderly man. "The railway line's at the end of that lane."

Bill felt suddenly afraid. "Railway line? Oh, no." He looked at his watch. "There's a train coming in five minutes!"

Bill rode Drover up to the blackberry hedge. He had no choice but to jump it. Nobody on foot could reach the little girl in time. He didn't think Drover had ever jumped anything as big and rough as this hedge. He cantered back a short way, turned, and set the mare at the tangled barrier.

Bonnie and Sam had raced to the bathrooms when they heard the scream. A crowd followed behind them. They came around the corner just as Bill and Drover galloped at the hedge.

"Go, Dad!" Sam yelled, as Drover flew over the blackberries.

The mare raced down the lane. The ground was rough and rutted, with snarls of blackberries reaching across it, but Drover didn't stumble. She tore toward the railway line faster than Bill thought she could move.

From close by came the *whooo hooo!* of the train.

"Come on, girl," Bill said to Drover. "Don't freak out at the train. I need you to be brave."

It seemed to take forever to reach the railway line. Each time the train whistled, Bill felt a cold hand clasp his heart. Suddenly Drover turned so fast that Bill had to hang on with everything he had.

He could see Kimberley ahead of him! She had pushed her trike onto the train tracks and was kicking it along with her chubby little legs.

Whooo hooo!

Bill glanced over his shoulder as Drover leaped up onto the tracks. The train was coming, closer and closer. Surely the driver could see him.

"Kimberley!" he shouted. "Get off the track!"

The toddler turned at the sound of her name and Bill shuddered to see how helpless she was. He urged Drover forward. Behind him, he could hear the squeal of the train's brakes.

The little girl looked up in terror as the horse galloped toward her.

Drover didn't shy away. It was as though she knew exactly what Bill needed to do. Bill leaned out of the saddle, way out and down. As Drover galloped past, he grabbed Kimberley by the back of her purple corduroy overalls and lifted her to safety.

Drover veered off the train tracks, scrambling down the bank like a cat, and slowed to a canter, then a stop, as the train roared safely past.

The train driver was leaning out his window, looking back. Bill gave him a wave to let him know everything was all right.

The little girl hadn't uttered a sound, but now she said, "Horsey."

"That's right," said Bill, settling her on the pommel of his saddle. "She's a wonderful horsey."

He could hear the cheer from the crowd at the showgrounds as soon as they turned down the lane. Drover walked quietly, sides heaving after the gallop. Kimberley babbled and laughed. Her parents raced toward them and Bill passed the little girl down. It was only then that he realized she was still sitting on her trike. When he'd scooped her up, she had held on to the plastic handlebars, and the trike had come with her.

Kimberley's parents kissed her and cuddled her, inspected her for cuts and scratches, and thanked Bill over and over. They walked back

along the lane to the showgrounds, with Bill
following on Drover. Kimberley kept turning in
her father's arms, calling, "Horsey, horsey," until
finally they passed her up to Bill and she rode
into the cheering crowd like a little princess.

A voice yelled out, "Three cheers for Bill
Cooper!" and everybody cheered him. Then
someone else yelled, "And three cheers for the
horse!" and they cheered Drover, too.

THE TRUTH

Sam tried to tell her father the truth about Drover that night. She lay on their saggy couch with Pants on her lap and listened as Bill told Smithy how brave his horse had been.

"She's been acting weird this week," he said into the phone. "It was like she'd forgotten everything she'd ever learned. I thought I might have to get rid of her, but, mate, you should have seen her today. What a star. She galloped in front of that train as cool as a cucumber."

He held the phone away from his ear and grinned at Sam as Smithy's squawks of disbelief echoed from the earpiece.

"I don't know what's changed her, but thank you. Thank you for a fantastic horse." Bill leaned back and stretched. "Yeah, you take care out on the road. We'll see you in the spring. Bye, mate."

"It's a different horse, Dad." The words were out of Sam's mouth before she'd even decided to say them. "This Drover is a brumby."

Bill looked down at his socks for a moment and then he roared with laughter. "Ha, ha, Sam. Very funny. My word, you're a trickster. You had me thinking there for a minute. Come on, let's get you into bed. It's been a huge day."

One Year Later . . .

It was the first day of summer vacation and it had rained for hours. Sam and Bonnie spent the whole afternoon inside, working on their horse scrapbooks. Bonnie drew a beautiful picture of the two of them double-dinking on Drover, and Sam wrote their names underneath. They rode the mare together all the time now, when Bill wasn't using her.

"I'm sick of being inside, Sam." Bonnie walked across to the window. "And look. It's stopped raining. Let's go for a ride."

The sun was just starting to set and the evening light made everything glow. Drover trotted up to meet them and Sam slipped the bridle over her ears.

"Remember how snooty the old Drover was?" Bonnie said as she rubbed the mare's ears. "Not like you, Miss Beautiful."

Drover seemed to smile, as though she understood. Maybe Bonnie really could talk Horse.

Sam swung up onto Drover's back, then
held her foot out rigid so Bon could use it as a
step. Drover's coat was still damp after the rain,
and the girls felt as though they were glued to
her. They rode down to the creek, with Pants
scouting ahead. Then they broke into an easy
canter and loped out of town, leaving the little
brown-and-white dog behind.

Drover's canter was smooth and unhurried,
and they let her choose her own way. She turned
up a bush track that wound into the foothills of
Wild Dog Range. Her stride quickened.

"We'd better not go too far," said Sam. "Dad
will go nuts if we're not home by dark."

Suddenly the track opened into a small
grassed valley surrounded by towering mountain
ash trees, their pale trunks ragged with bark.
Drover stopped still, listening, then whinnied.
Her neigh rang around the clearing like a siren.

"She's calling the brumbies," Bonnie
whispered into Sam's ear. "Maybe she wants to
go back to them."

Drover's ears were pricked, quivering. From
high above came the noise of creatures moving
fast through the bush. A whinny floated down.
They could hear the horses getting closer. Then,
there they were, on the far side of the valley,

twelve brumbies standing nervously together in
the evening gloom.

Drover felt liked a coiled spring under the
girls, as though she might explode in an instant.

"I'm scared, Sam," Bonnie whispered. "Do you
think we should get off?"

"No, we'll be okay. Relax. Trust her. Remember,
she chose to live with us. I don't think she wants
to go back to the mountains."

A silver gray horse stepped away from the mob and moved toward them.

"I bet that's old Drover," Sam whispered so quietly that Bon only just caught her words. "It's gotta be, don't you think?"

Bon squeezed Sam's waist. "Look! She's got a foal."

The mare came right up to them, nickering softly. The two silvery horses stood shoulder to shoulder, sniffing each other. Sam leaned slowly across and lifted the brumby's mane. It was tangled, now, after a year in the bush. The moon-shaped scar showed dark against the silver coat.

"It is her! It's Dad's old Drover."

Bonnie squeezed Sam so hard she couldn't breathe. "Now we know for sure. Our horse switch theory is right!"

The brumbies suddenly turned back into the bush and old Drover wheeled to chase them. Her dark foal followed at her side.

Bonnie and Sam sat on their Drover, the horse that had chosen not to be a brumby, and listened to the wild horses moving off through the bush.

"We'd better go," Bonnie said in a tiny voice. But before Sam even gathered the reins, Drover turned away from her old life and headed back along the track toward home.

All the house lights were on as they cantered through Currawong Creek. Anyone looking out would have seen only blackness, but Bonnie's and Sam's eyes were used to the dark. They raced up the track to Sam's house, night riders with a secret.